Isabella,
Aiden,
and Collin,
and the 2nd
Enjoy
Mystery!,
L. P. Chase
11/2/11

Elliot Stone

and the Mystery of the
Backyard Treasure

By L.P. Chase

Illustrations by Kara Elsberry

Copyright © 2008 by L. P. Chase

Cover design being used with permission from Rain Publishing, Inc."

ISBN 0-7414-4804-1

Published by:

INFI(∞)ITY
PUBLISHING.COM

1094 New DeHaven Street, Suite 100
West Conshohocken, PA 19428-2713
Info@buybooksontheweb.com
www.buybooksontheweb.com
Toll-free (877) BUY BOOK
Local Phone (610) 941-9999
Fax (610) 941-9959

Printed in the United States of America

Printed on Recycled Paper

Published

For Bud,

who always used to say,

"I hope you're writing this stuff down."

I finally did.

Rest in peace.

-LPC-

Acknowledgments

I'd like to express my sincere appreciation to a few special people. First, I'd like to thank Fernando (Nando) Pica, owner of Aiello Bros Pork Stores, Inc. located in Centereach, New York. Nando took time out of his busy schedule to sit with me and answer all my questions regarding wine cellars, the aging of provolone cheese, and the process of drying sausages. The factual knowledge I gained made *The Backyard Treasure* much more authentic.

Next, I'd like to thank Mr. Joseph Buscemi, for his helpful input in my research on the aging and drying process as well.

Additionally, I'd like to express my gratitude to Joyce Gilmour for helping me create a thought provoking Elliot Quiz in the back of the book.

Finally, I'd like to thank my husband and family for their continued support of my writing endeavors. I couldn't have done this without you.

Table of Contents

CHAPTER ONE

The Dreaded Black Bag

Hi, remember me? My name is Elliot Stone, and I'm in the fourth grade. The last time we met, I was in a real pickle. Thanks to my best friends, Jake Weber and Cassie Hawthorne, I was able to solve the biggest mystery of my life. You know, the one where my mom was turning into an alien. Well, I'm really glad that's over. But not long after that happened, we stumbled on another baffling mystery. Jake, Cassie, and I were about to embark on our next mission.

The rain was crashing down, making weird drum sounds on the air conditioner in my window. I could have sworn it sounded like someone's fingers tapping. My bedroom is on the second floor, so unless the guy was about twenty feet tall, I doubt anyone was out there. But, I peeked out through the slats of my mini-blinds anyway—just to make sure.

I was so hung up on the sound the rain was making, I almost forgot how freaked out I was about the creepy statue I had seen when I was at my grandparents' house the night before. My grandparents live around the corner from us, so we go there all the time. Well, as soon as I walked into the living room, there in plain sight on the bookshelf, was the most evil-looking statue I had ever seen. It was a dark and shriveled little head with its eyes and mouth sewn shut. I shuddered at the look of it. My grandfather said it wasn't real—that it was just a souvenir from an old friend. But I wasn't sure I believed him. I couldn't even look at it long enough to decide if it was real or fake. The thing was so eerie, I had to get out of the room. All I could think about the whole time was calling Jake and telling him what I saw, but we got home too late.

The rain pounded my air conditioner even harder. I wasn't allowed to call Jake until I was finished cleaning. Saturday mornings at my house are for dusting, vacuuming, and putting tons of clothes away. It's the worst day of the week—at least until the rooms are done. I hate cleaning my room! I think I hate cleaning my room more than anything else in the entire world, well, anything else in the world *except* touching the kitchen sponge—that totally grosses me out. But I'll save that story for another time.

Anyway, I think I must've walked back and forth from the window to my closet to my desk about a hundred times. I needed to produce some results fast or my mother would be coming up with the dreaded black bag.

Do you know what the dreaded black bag is? Well, if I don't keep my room neat, my mother will come whizzing through my door like a vicious tornado sucking up everything in her path in about five seconds and then toss all of it in her black garbage bag—the bag that sucks up every cool thing you ever wanted to save, or every treasure you'd ever found. It's more like a black hole if you ask me. I would do almost anything to avoid that scene.

The problem is I have to make my room look like I cleaned it, but I'm not good at that because I like to save everything.

"Elliot," she called up the stairs. "Are you working on that room of yours?"

"Yeah, I'm, uh, almost done," I answered quickly so she wouldn't make the loud, stomping trek up the stairs. I call it the "Trek of Doom." You can hear every footstep getting louder and coming closer until you know you're doomed.

"Almost done?" I asked myself. "I'm not even close." One by one, I picked little things that I loved out of my junk drawer, like old rusty nails, pieces of electronic pc boards, broken shells from the beach, bird feathers, and screws that I might need for something someday. As I carefully evaluated each piece, I made the decision that these were all very important and I *had* to keep them. Back in the drawer they went. I obviously wasn't getting anywhere with this cleaning thing. I needed a bigger room. Every kid needs at least five junk drawers, don't ya think?

I was dying to tell Jake about the creepy statue I had seen, so I started to hurry up. I grabbed at a pile of dirty clothes on the floor. It was the overflow pile from my hamper. As I pulled the clothes toward me, I noticed an old tin treasure box taking a ride on my jeans. I must've tossed it in the corner and forgotten all about it, which isn't too hard to believe since it was behind the clothes hamper. Who looks back *there*? Anyway, it was some old box that my grandfather had given my dad when he was a kid. Even though it was a little dented and didn't close the way it was supposed to, it was still pretty neat. The blue and silver designs and metal latch made it look like a real treasure chest.

Then, I came up with a plan. I decided I would put all my favorite things in that box so my mom wouldn't throw them out. I started across the room when I stepped on a board game and crushed the corner of the box. "Ow, ow, ow," I yelled, grabbing my foot. I cringed as all the pieces shot around the room like little torpedoes. "Oh, crud!" I mumbled, looking at the new, improved mess.

Well, at that point, it didn't take a rocket scientist to see that my room was a complete disaster. I picked up the tin box and began imagining what I could put in it. That's when I came up with an even better idea. Jake and I could bury the box in the backyard somewhere, like a real treasure. *I'm brilliant!* I thought. *I can't wait to tell Jake.*

"What's that, Elliot?" interrupted the annoying voice of my little sister through the crack in my door.

"What do you want, Sammy? Shouldn't you be cleaning *YOUR* room or something?" I grumbled, rolling my eyes. Sammy pushed her way into the room and sat on my rug anyway.

"Get out of here. You're wrecking everything."

"I'm just watching," she said.

"Watching what?" I rolled my eyes harder, huffing this time. "Whatever!" I didn't have time to fight with her. The clock was ticking and my room wasn't getting any cleaner.

When I had my most important items in the box, I decided to sneak a call to Jake and fill him in about the creepy statue and see if he wanted to bury some treasure with me. I hurried up, tossing around the mangled sheets and blankets on my bed to find where I put my walkie-talkie. Really, they were Jake's walkie-talkies. We each had one—it was our only way to secretly communicate. As much as I hated using those superhero walkie-talkies, it was all we had

. . . for now. I couldn't wait for Jake to get his new, more mature pair of secret communication devices like he'd promised. Then suddenly, I saw the antenna sticking out from under my pillow and I grabbed it.

I almost forgot Sammy was still sitting on the floor watching me. "Do you mind?" I finally demanded, motioning with my hands for her to get lost. And as I pressed the little red button to call Jake, my worst nightmare became a reality. I heard the beginning of the "Trek of Doom."

"Elliot, if I come up there and that room hasn't been cleaned . . ." *Boom. **Boom.** **BOOM.***

I flung the walkie-talkie out of my hands, and it smashed into the wall. Sammy screamed and darted out of my room, slamming the door shut behind her. I ran around in a panic to find a hiding spot for the box.

My body was vibrating like a motor when . . . *quick, under the bed,* I thought. I kicked the box under with my foot and CRASH! The door flew open hitting the wall behind it with another huge bang.

"Ahhhh!" I screamed. "You scared me, Mom!" I said in a goofy voice, trying to make her laugh.

"That's it, Elliot!" was all she said without even moving her lips. "I'm not laughing." The words came slithering through her teeth.

I gulped. I knew what was coming next. She proceeded to open that big black bag without saying another word and raided each pile like a dinosaur attacking its prey—staring and clawing and grabbing. Clink, clank, crash was all I heard. "Look at this," she mumbled under her breath. "How do you let it get like this?"

I saw Sammy peeking in from the hallway, but I knew if I yelled for her to get out of there, I'd be in bigger trouble. My mom continued to rummage through my things without stopping. I looked up with the cutest face possible, but she didn't even look back. *Well, that didn't work,* I thought. She kept her eyes fixed straight ahead of her as she dumped one thing after the other into the bag. I kept gulping to keep myself from saying something stupid and praying that she wouldn't throw out anything good.

It was no use. I couldn't control myself. "Wait, Mom, not those!" I scooped up some marbles before she could get them. "Hold on, I need that too." I grabbed a shredded old piece of my first baby blanket.

"What on earth are you saving that for?" she said, looking at me like I was nuts.

"I just want to keep it," I said, stuffing it in my pocket. But my mom didn't skip a beat. She grabbed some more things and stuffed them into the bag.

"Hold it! Hold it! I have to keep that." I plucked an old key out of her hands.

"And why would you—"

"I collect old keys."

"You and your father," she said shaking her head. "What on earth will you do with old useless keys?"

The sound of crumpling, clanking, and plunking echoed in my head until the attack was over—the calm after the storm. I had pools of water doing a balancing act on the edges of my eyelids. The slightest movement would have caused a flood of tears to gush down my face, so I was careful not even to blink. Crying was definitely not the answer here.

When my mother left, half my room went with her. I bid farewell to all those pieces of me—all that neat stuff, odd-looking buttons, old candy from birthday party goody bags, and ceramic figures I painted when I was five. All of it . . . gone! I felt a little empty, but, wow! My room looked so clean! I could finally walk around without stepping on something. I could even open my drawers. What a concept! The "Trek of Doom" actually turned out to be a good thing this time and, besides, my mother never found my treasure box.

Now it was definitely time to call Jake. We needed to have a serious meeting. We had a sinister looking statue to investigate and a treasure box to bury. But first I had to confer with Jake and see if he wanted to put anything in the box, and more importantly, we had to come up with the perfect place to bury it.

CHAPTER TWO

A New Plan

I pressed the little red button. "Jake, are you there? Jake?" I whispered. I was pressing my lips against the walkie-talkie so hard, I didn't realize I was spitting all over the speaker. "Oh snap! How disgusting!" I said under my breath. I started looking for something to wipe off the spit, when I heard crackling and static and then Jake's broken-up voice. Shhh, ccchhh, "It's me," said Jake. I hurried to wipe off the speaker with my sleeve because nothing was left in my room to wipe it off with, not even a dirty sock.

"Jake, can you meet me at the tree house today? I think we have a new mission, but I can't meet you until later. I just got in big trouble because of my room being a mess—"

"Surprise, surprise," he interrupted me, laughing. "Way to go." Shhh, ccchhh.

"Hey, c'mon. It wasn't that bad . . . was it?" I knew the answer to that question.

"Uh, do you want the truth, or do you just want me to make you feel better?" Shhh, ccchhh.

"Just make me feel better," I said, with a laugh.

"Okay, then it wasn't that bad," he went along with me. "Now what's this new mission?"

First, I had to walk closer to the window because the static was getting so loud it was annoying. Either the batteries were going bad, or the rain was messing up our connec-

tion. "My grandfather has a gross-looking statue of a miniature head in his living room."

"Get out of here. You mean like a shrunken head?"

"Yeah, that's it! Exactly! It's a shrunken head. You
gotta come to their house with me and see this thing. You'll
totally freak."

"Okay, tell me when," Jake agreed. I could practically feel his excitement through the walkie-talkie.

"Wait, there's more. I have this old tin box that I put
some things in, you know, important stuff. I want to bury it
someplace, sorta like a treasure chest. What do ya think?"

"Oh that's pretty cool! But where do you wanna bury
it?" Jake wondered.

"That's what we have to figure out. Wanna make all
the plans at the tree house later?"

"Okay, I'll see if I have anything to put in it too."
Shhh, ccchhh.

"All right, but this static is so annoying, so let's talk more at the tree house. I'll see if I can meet you there after lunch."

"Okay, Elliot, over and out."

"Will you stop with that over and out stuff?" I begged, but Jake had already turned his walkie-talkie off.

I started downstairs when Sammy burst through her bedroom door and ran over to me.

"Elliot, did you get in big trouble? *I* didn't get in trouble. *My* room is clean. Did Mommy throw any of *your* stuff out?" she rambled behind me.

"Will you stop following me? Man, you're a pain!" I shook my head. It didn't matter. She stayed one step behind me the whole way downstairs.

I had to find a way to make up for my room so my mom would let me go to the tree house. When I got into the kitchen, my dad was reading the newspaper and my mom was feeding my new baby brother, Tommy. *Whew! I'm saved,* I thought. My mom had been a little edgy since Tommy arrived, but at least she was always in a good mood when she was feeding him. Tommy was spitting mashed food all over the place. Nasty! There's nothing worse then half-eaten baby food squirting back out at you.

"Hey, little buddy," I said to Tommy, as he turned his carrot-covered face toward me. His hands and feet started wiggling around, and I think he even smiled at me.

"I think he knows you already," Mom said, scraping the spoon around his mouth to catch all that food leaking out. Maybe she'd forgotten she was even mad at me.

Looking at him, I felt all mushy inside. Tommy is really cute, but I have to admit, I still stare at him sometimes and wonder, *Could you be an alien?* Nah. I poured some milk and mumbled a lame apology to my mom.

"What's that, Elliot?" she asked, raising her left eyebrow.

"I'm sorry about before, I-I mean, my room and all."
I was looking down into the cup in case I had to blink back
tears again.

"Elliot's sorry, Mom," Sammy interrupted. "That's
what he said . . . he's sorry."

I looked over at Sammy with the evil eye. Dad
glanced up over his eyeglasses glaring at me and scared my
evil eye right back into its socket. Ya don't have to tell me
twice. After all, I was trying to weasel my way out of trouble
and get down to the tree house to meet Jake.

"I know you're sorry," my mom said, but you really
have to start being more responsible. I'm not going to clean
that room anymore. Next time, I'll throw everything out, and
I mean EVERYTHING!" This time she got loud. And I
mean LOUD.

"Okay, I'm *really* sorry," I said. I meant it that time.
Now, I had to make my move. I started clearing the table and

putting the dishes in the sink. I threw all the napkins in the garbage pail and started tying up the bag.

"What are you up to?" Dad blew my cover, flipping the page of his newspaper.

"Nothing." I shook my head trying not to smile. *I've been snagged again,* I thought. "Can I go up to the tree house for a little while? Jake's meeting me there," I asked with a toothy grin.

My parents looked across the table at each other and my mom shook her head. I knew if I looked at her long enough, she would smile. It worked like a charm! She did smile, still shaking her head, and said, "Get outta here. You drive me crazy."

"How come Elliot always gets to do everything?" Sammy whined.

I ran out of the kitchen before they could change their minds. Taking three steps at a time, I reached the top of the stairs and tripped, flying into my room like a pebble out of a slingshot. Figured. Well, the rug burn wasn't too bad. I brushed off my elbows and grabbed my walkie-talkie and top-secret backpack. You know, the one with my purple notebook. I always take it to the tree house when we have a mission to work on.

As I flew through the kitchen toward the front door, my dad called out, "Don't be too long Elliot. We're going to Grandma's house for dinner."

"Can Jake come too?" I figured I'd ask. How much more trouble could I get into?

"I guess. If it's okay with his parents," my mom gave in. "He's practically part of the family by now."

"Yes! You rock, Mom!" I looked over at Sammy and did a little dance. "Oh yeah, oh yeah, you rock, you rock!"

"Mom!" Sammy shrieked.

"Elliot!"

I grabbed my stuff and busted out of the front door before my luck ran out. I threw my backpack over the handlebars of my bike and took a running jump-start down the driveway. Whoosh! I went flying down the hill and started pedaling as fast as I could toward the end of the block. I almost killed myself because the ground was still wet from the major rain we had that morning.

I looked around to see if Jake had arrived yet. There was no sign of his bike, which was kind of strange. He never walks anywhere. I gathered my stuff and tried to lean my bike on the bushes, but it kept falling over. I finally gave up and just pushed it on its side. The kickstand on that stupid thing never worked anyway. I hustled up to the entrance of the tree house and grabbed the rope. I hated getting rope burn and little splinters, but I hoisted myself up anyway and started climbing up the steps to the door. I rubbed my hands, examining them for any spiky little splinters and then tapped out the secret code on the door.

"Tap, tap, tap, pause, tap, pause, tap."

"Is that you?" Jake's voice called out, a little out of breath.

"Yeah, open up," I said, struggling with my backpack. "My hands are falling off."

Jake opened the door, gasping for breath, and hi-fived me as I pushed in past him. I gave him a look and plopped down on the beanbag chair.

"What's with you?" I asked.

"My bike's broken . . . so I had to run all the way here . . . and I can barely breathe," he said holding his chest.

"Oh, get over it, Jake," I said laughing. "You only live a block away, you big baby."

"Whoa, that was harsh."

"Now, listen, I have a plan with this box." I pulled out the treasure box and showed it to Jake.

"Hey, this thing is cool. Where'd you get it again?" he asked checking out the blue and silver cover.

"It was my dad's when he was a kid. I've had it for-ever. But when I was cleaning my room today, my mom almost threw out everything I owned. So I had to stash my best junk in here. Did you bring stuff to put in it?" I asked him.

"Yeah, are you kidding?" Jake said as he emptied his pockets. "I've been looking for things to put in it since you beeped me on the walkie-talkie." He pulled out crumpled-up foreign money, an awesome skeleton ring with two ruby eyes in it, and a folded-up piece of paper.

"Wait, what's that?" I asked, grabbing the paper from him. I unfolded it. "A heart with a name on it? What's this? Whose name is that?"

Jake turned beet red and grabbed it right back. "For-get it," he said. "Just forget it."

"All right, I didn't see a thing. So now, my mom said if you're allowed, you could come with us to my grandparents' house for dinner later. You wanna bury the box over there? You know their yard. It's huge."

"That's perfect, Elliot, then Sammy won't be trying to dig it up on us. She could ruin the whole thing if we bury it in your yard."

"Nice thinking," I said, high-fiving Jake again.

"And what about the weird statue?" Jake asked. "What's up with that?"

"I don't know. We'll have to investigate that when we get there. It's in the living room on the bookshelf. So let's try to get a closer look."

"Okay," Jake said hesitantly.

"Great!" Then it's a plan. We'll get to my grandparents' house and do the usual hello stuff, then we'll check out the statue. After that, we can map out our digging spot for the treasure box."

"Sounds good to me," Jake said.

I started writing some notes in my purple notebook:

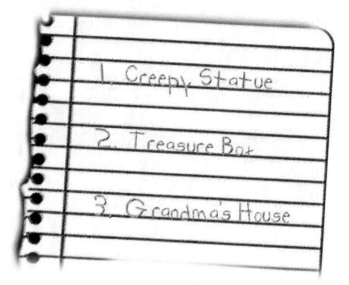

We packed up the box with all our treasures and I tossed it all in my top-secret backpack. Then we double-checked the bicycle lock on the door and hurried down the rickety steps. I started to hop on my bike. "Hey, Jake, you want a ride? I wouldn't want you to gasp all the way home, now," I said, coughing and grabbing my chest. I pretended like I was falling over.

"Hey . . . wait a minute . . ." Jake started laughing. He jumped on the back and I practically had to stand up to get the bike moving.

"Man, you're heavy," I said, getting a well-deserved wallop on the back of the head. We laughed all the way up the block.

CHAPTER THREE

The Box Burial

"Hello, boys," my grandmother greeted us at the front door. "Jimmy, the kids are here," she called out to my grandfather." She planted a hard kiss on my cheek first, then

Jake's. He glanced up at me, pleading for help as she squeezed the guts out of him with one of those famous grandma hugs.

"You're on your own, buddy." I put my hands up. "Just go with the flow." As soon as we started to go into the house, Sammy came barreling through us.

"Sammy, will you watch it!"

"Hi Grandma. Grandma, look," Sammy kept talking. "Look at my doll. Mommy helped me make this dress for her. It matches the one I have on. See?"

That's when we made a run for it. Ever since my little brother, Tommy, was born, Sammy had turned into a major pain. She was searching for attention and knew my grandmother would spend a long time ooh-ing and aah-ing for her. So we bolted. We dropped our stuff in the hallway and headed into the living room to say hello to my grandfather. As soon as we turned the corner, Jake stopped dead in his tracks and I smashed right into him.

"What are you doing?" I asked him.

"What the——?" Jake looked at me like he had just seen a ghost. "Is that what you were talking about?" Jake whispered, pointing to the gruesome statue.

"Hey there, boys. What's happening?" Grandpa said, slowly walking over to us.

"Hey, Gramps," I said and prepared for the death-grip handshake. "So what's that thing again?" I asked, pointing to the shriveled up brown head. I looked over at Jake again. He backed up from the bookshelf a few steps. "That was never here before."

"Oh, you like that?" Grandpa said laughing. "It's just a replica of an old shrunken head. Heh, heh."

"So where'd you get it? And, uh . . . why on earth would you want it in your living room?"

"An old friend of mine sent it as a souvenir from his trip to the Amazon," he said, amused by the whole thing.

"When we were young boys, we were fascinated with shrunken heads. You two wanna hear some good stories?"

"No way!" I said. "And if you ask me, the whole thing is kind of weird, isn't it, Jake?" Jake was still staring at the evil statue. He nodded in agreement as I turned the face toward the wall. "It's creeping me out!"

"Ah, you boys have to toughen up," Grandpa said as he turned toward the hall.

Grandma walked into the living room, bouncing Tommy in her arms. He was holding a rattle and trying to get it in his mouth, but instead he kept bopping himself in the head. We were all busy paying attention to him for a few minutes while my parents were doting on Sammy.

"Why don't you kids go play?" Grandma said. "Dinner won't be ready for a little while." That was our cue. In less than three seconds, we grabbed our stuff from the hallway, charged through the kitchen, and made it to the back door. As we headed outside, my grandfather followed us through the kitchen. I could have sworn he said, "Hey, Frannie, I'm going to visit the dungeon for a minute."

"Hey, did he just say he was going to the dungeon?" Jake asked, scratching his head.

"Nah, we probably heard it wrong. Besides, people don't have dungeons anymore . . . right?"

"I hope not," Jake said as the back door slammed behind us.

"At least it stopped raining," I said, trying to change the subject.

We went over to the fence on the side of the house and looked around the yard for a good hiding place. We decided to start at the tenth picket of the fence, take ten giant steps forward, and start digging. That way, we would remember exactly where we buried the box so we could dig it up again later. It was foolproof. Most of the side yard was dirt. A few scattered plugs of crab grass stuck up, but that was all. It was a little muddy from the morning's rain, but not too bad. Some patches were still a little hard, so we decided to use some of our tools to soften it.

"These should help make digging easier. Here. Use this." I handed Jake a hammer, pointing to the hooked end. I took the screwdriver and we jabbed them in and out of the dirt to make our job easier. Then we used small shovels and dug in three or four different spots before we could make a good hole. "Let's make it really deep," I suggested.

We finally dug a giant hole and were ready for the box burial. "Let's hurry before Sammy comes out and sees us." As soon as I got the words out, the faint voice of my grandmother came from around the house.

"Boys, dinner is ready."

"Oh man!" I opened up my backpack as fast as I could and took out the box. First, we made sure all our stuff was in it. "Yep, got everything." Then I made sure to close the latch tightly before we positioned it perfectly in the hole. We started dumping muddy clumps of dirt on top until the treasure box was completely covered. Jake and I jumped up and down, pounding the entire area to make it look like nothing had happened. What we really looked like was a bunch of monkeys bouncing up and down in circles. Sneaker prints were everywhere.

"What on earth happened to you two boys?" my grandmother asked when we got to the back door. "Don't take another step. Off with those sneakers. And you'd better go wash up, dinner is on the table."

We practically inhaled dinner. My grandmother makes the best lasagna in the world. And meatballs too, but I couldn't say that in front of my mom. She likes for hers to be the best.

"Good lasagna, Grandma," I said, staying neutral. My grandfather opened a bottle of wine and everyone was talking about its bouquet and full body. Then they moved on to how great the dried sausage was . . . blah . . . blah . . . blah. Sometimes grown-ups talk about the most boring things at the dinner table or, even worse, laugh about stupid things that I don't think are funny. I tried not to pay much attention. Instead, I messed around. First I tried picking sesame seeds off the bread and flicking them across the table at Sammy. She never noticed. Then I started on Jake. He was shoving entire meatballs in his mouth. "Take human bites," I whispered, kicking him under the table. "You have to *breathe* in between forkfuls," I said, trying to get him laughing. One time, I actually made Jake laugh so hard that soda came shooting out of his nose. Now that was beautiful. I don't think he wanted to repeat it, though, so he managed to grab a napkin and cover his whole face just in case.

When everyone was finished, my mom got up and helped my grandma clear the table. Dad was holding Tommy while Sammy kissed him on the head and pinched his cheeks about a million times. "You're gonna suffocate him, Sam. Leave him alone!"

"He likes it. I'm his favorite," Sammy said, sticking her tongue out at me. Just then, Tommy's arms swung around and hit her smack in the nose. Sammy started crying and Jake and I started cracking up. That's when my grandmother chimed in and asked us to do her a favor. I think she was just trying to keep us out of trouble. She's great at that.

"Can you boys go downstairs to the basement and grab a few cans of my peaches? They're on the back of the stainless steel shelving. You might have to move around a few things. I'll make a nice peach cobbler for dessert."

"Sure, Grandma." We went down the hallway to the basement door. I don't know about you, but all basements are creepy to me. "You go first," I told Jake. "I hate going down here."

"It's *your* grandmother's house. *You* go first."

We decided to go down at the same time, bumping into each other the whole way. My grandparents' basement was pretty organized; at least we didn't trip over old toys and boxes and stuff like we do at my house. Most things were covered in plastic. It even smelled like mothballs down there.

We got to the canning shelf and started moving things around. It wasn't so bad. "Here are the pickles. Here are the tomatoes," I said, moving more cans on the shelves. "Oh, here are the peaches." Jake stood right next to me, tapping his fingers on his legs. All of a sudden, we heard a faint thump behind the shelf. Then came another thump and another and then a huge one.

"Ahhhh," Jake screamed and crashed into me. I fell backward and slammed into the shelf, knocking over a bunch of boxes.

"What the heck was that?" Jake said, all freaked out.

"How am I supposed to know? I'm on the floor. You gonna just leave me here?" I asked. Jake started to run toward the stairs. "Hey wait," I said. "Get back here and help me fix this before we go up."

The Box Burial

We started picking up the boxes and standing them at the back of the shelf when Jake and I noticed something weird at exactly the same time. On the wall behind the canning shelf, we saw some kind of weird miniature door, but it had no doorknob.

Jake backed up again, slowly. "We should go now."

"Wait," I said, rubbing my fingers over the dusty wood, "Doesn't that look like a keyhole? What do you think is back there?"

"Maybe that's the dungeon your grandfather was talking about. Shrunken heads? Dungeons? I'm outta here." Jake bolted, tripping over his own feet until he got to the stairs.

"Hold on, Jake. There's no such thing as a dungeon. It's just a plain old basement," I yelled out, and then I looked back at the door. I heard another thump and decided to run with Jake toward the stairs.

We started taking two steps at a time when I realized I had forgotten the peaches. "Come back with me, Jake."

"No way! Are you crazy?"

"All right, wait here . . . and don't you dare move!" My heart was pounding as I sprinted back to the shelf, grabbed the cans, and got back to Jake. We sounded like two hyenas half-screaming, half-laughing as we scrambled to the top of the stairs. I felt like someone was chasing us. "I have a feeling this is gonna need further investigation," I said, gasping for breath. "What do you think?"

Jake didn't look so happy. We decided first thing the next day, we would tell Cassie. It looked like the three of us definitely had a new mission on our hands.

CHAPTER FOUR

The Sleeping Willow

"Please take your seats," Mrs. Pendleton said.

I can't believe I got her for the second year in a row.

First third grade, now fourth. But this year, Jake, Cassie, and

I were lucky enough to be in the same class.

"Here comes Cassie," I whispered to Jake. "Quick!

Hold up the note."

Cassie's eyes practically sprang out of her head when she read our note. She loves this detective stuff.

"Cassie, Jake, Elliot!" Mrs. Pendleton warned us. "Save it for later."

Cassie cupped her hand over her mouth pursing her lips. "Tell me at recess, under the Sleeping Willow."

We met in front of the giant weeping willow tree on the side of the baseball field. It had fallen down during a major hurricane last year, but the roots stayed attached so it still blooms. The tree is practically lying on the ground, so we started calling it the Sleeping Willow. It's sort of like a tent now with the twisty vines hanging all the way down to the ground. We moved the branches apart and went inside. "It's so cool in here, isn't it?" I said, looking around.

"So what have you got? What's this new mission?" Cassie got serious right away.

I took out my purple notebook and flipped to my latest entry. "Jake and I buried this old box in my grandparents' yard yesterday—"

"Why'd you do that?" she interrupted.

"Just wait. Let me finish. When we got there, my grandfather had this creepy-looking statue in the living room—he said it was a replica of a shrunken head from the Amazon."

"Yeah, so I still don't get the mission," Cassie said.

"Don't worry, there's more."

"Lots more," Jake added, nodding his head. "Lots more!"

"First let me write this down . . ."

4. Shrunken head

"Now, where was I? Oh, yeah, when Jake and I were going out to the yard, we could have sworn we heard my grandfather say he was going down to the dungeon."

"Yeah, and?" Cassie asked.

"Did you hear me? He said DUNGEON!"

"So, that's no big deal. Lots of people call their basement the dungeon. Didn't you ever hear that?"

"Okay, Miss Know-it-all, then, how do you explain that freaky, secret mini-door?" Jake blurted—his eyes twice their normal size.

"Uh, what freaky, secret mini-door?" Cassie got a little nervous.

"When we went down to get peaches, Jake practically knocked over the whole shelf—"

"Me? What about you?"

" . . . and that's when we noticed the little door. It's kind of beat-up and old looking, and there's no doorknob, just a weird keyhole. And we heard thumping noises coming from inside."

I started writing again . . .

5. Dungeon

6. Freaky, secret mini-door

7. Thumping

"Okay, guys, so it sounds like we might have a new mission. We have some good clues to start with, so let's make a plan." Cassie helped to orchestrate our next moves.

"Wait, what is this box thing you were telling me about?" she asked.

"I totally forgot. I have this old box from when my dad was a kid. Jake and I put some treasures and stuff in it and buried it in my grandparents' backyard, like a treasure chest."

"That sounds kind of cool," Cassie said. "Can I put something in it? I have a really neat genie lamp necklace. That would be perfect!"

"Yeah, sure. We mapped out exactly where we buried it—ten giant steps forward from the tenth picket in the fence. We can dig it up later after school," I told her.

"So what are we really dealing with, Elliot?" Jake backtracked. "Do you think your grandfather has something weird going on? Shrunken heads, dungeons . . . the whole thing is freakin' me out!" Jake's voice cracked.

I just shrugged. I couldn't even imagine. "We'll check out that statue again later and start looking for any clues in the house. Maybe we can go down in the basement again and look around."

"Are you nuts?" Jake panicked.

"I have an idea," Cassie broke in again. "Why don't I do some research on shrunken heads, just to prove they're not real."

She loves doing research. Weird, I know, but she does. "Go ahead, brainiac. Do your thing," I told her. "I have enough homework. I don't need to sign up for another research project." Then I asked, "So, do we have a mission?" I put my hand out first. Jake put his hand on mine and Cassie put hers on top.

"The deal is sealed!"

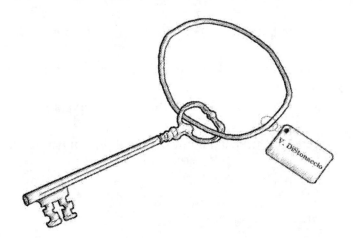

CHAPTER FIVE

V. DiStonaccio

I got to my grandparents' house first.

"Hey Grandma," I called from the street. She was sweeping the driveway. I think I have the only grandmother in the world who sweeps cement. "Is it okay if my friends meet me here to hang out in the yard for a little while? Jake and I were messing around in the dirt back there yesterday, remember?"

"Of course, honey, just don't bother with the pile of rocks on the side. Your grandfather just had a truckload of pea gravel delivered this morning for his garden."

"We won't touch it. Don't worry."

"It's so nice to have you boys over. It puts some life into this quiet old house. Would you like a snack, dear? I'll go in and fix you something."

"Nah. Thanks, I'll wait for Jake and Cassie. Oh! Here's Jake now." Jake's bike turned the corner and headed up the driveway where we were standing.

"You're riding your bike? I thought it was broken."

"My dad fixed it yesterday while I was having dinner with you guys." Jake answered. He looked up at my grandmother and gave a little wave.

"Hello, Jake dear. How are you?"

"Hi." He cringed.

I think he was staying on his bike a little longer, hoping to avoid the grandma hug, but she came over and smashed a good kiss on his cheek anyway and then messed up his hair. I pointed at him and mouthed a big laugh from behind her back.

"Well, you boys let me know when you're hungry and, remember, don't upset your grandfather's gravel."

"Gravel? What gravel?" Jake whispered to me as she went into the house.

"Oh, some pea gravel they had delivered this morning for the garden. We're not supposed to bother it."

"That's weird. Who buys gravel in the fall? Aren't the plants all about to die soon anyway?" Jake wondered as we headed into the yard.

"I never really thought about it. I guess it is kinda strange. Whatever." Just then, I saw Cassie coming up the driveway and waved her over. "We're back here, Cassie," I called from the fence.

"Elliot, Jake, you guys are not gonna believe this!" Cassie parked her bike and came running up to the gate. "Let me in, let me in," she said, shaking the gate impatiently.

"What's going on, Cass?" I asked, as I unlatched it to let her in. She pushed past me, waving a bunch of papers around.

"I did some research when I got home from school. I found out there IS such a thing as shrunken heads. They did it back in the nineteenth century in South America. Some tribes in the Amazon used to take the heads of their enemies. And people, you know, tourists would go and buy them as collectibles, so the government had to ban them because the more they bought, the more heads were made." She was chewing her nails down to little nubs.

I never saw Cassie get her feathers ruffled. She's usually the calm one. "Okay, okay. Maybe we should put that away for now," I suggested. "Let's go dig up the treasure box and put your stuff in it."

"But, Elliot, it's so messed up. I hate when I read too much. I don't want to know this stuff. You know what they did? They used gravel and pebbles, and boiling water, and it's totally disgustingly gross."

My legs went numb when she said that. My stomach sank about ten feet, and I thought I was about to throw up. "Did you say gravel and pebbles?" I squeaked.

Jake and I looked at each other and screamed at the same time. Then Cassie screamed too. "What? What? Will you tell me what's going on?"

"C-Cassie," Jake started. "Elliot's grandmother just told us not to go near the pile of pea gravel on the side of the house, th-that it was delivered this morning for his grandfather's g- garden."

We watched the color drain out of Cassie's face. She stood paralyzed with her mouth opened wide. We started pacing. Jake was scratching his head and Cassie just stood there, white as a sheet, holding her research papers.

"Wait . . . wait . . . wait." I had to get hold of myself. "We can't start panicking yet. Let's be sensible." I took my purple notebook out of the backpack and jotted this latest newsflash:

8. Gravel delivery for shrunken heads

An eerie chill ran through me as I made the entry, but I didn't let it show. I told them I thought we should go dig up the box and take care of that first. Then we could try to process this whole gravel issue. Cassie and Jake agreed with me. We walked over to the tenth picket and started taking ten giant steps forward. Since I'm taller than Jake, and he's taller than Cassie, we all landed in different spots. We knelt down and grabbed our tools. For a moment, there was silence. The wind blew around some dried leaves and the cool air felt good on my sweaty face. I started digging.

"Go deeper," Jake said.

We couldn't find the box. I moved to another spot. "No box here. What about your spot, Jake?"

"I'm not sure yet." He dug and dug some more. "I can't believe we can't find that stupid box. We only buried it yesterday. How can that be?"

Cassie was busily putting on rubber gloves and goggles.

"Are you kidding me, Cass? Come on!" Jake rolled his eyes.

"I'm not about to get filthy like you two," she said.

The three of us didn't give up. We kept moving a few inches to different areas and digging some more, when suddenly my shovel hit something—Clunk! "Did you guys hear that? I think I found it."

Cassie got excited. She took out her genie lamp necklace and a few other things to put in the box. Jake and I started clawing at the dirt with our hands to get to it. The sun was beginning to go down as the sky turned into dusk. We pushed over the dirt until we finally saw the cover of the box.

"Here it is," Jake yelled. The three of us were looking into the hole as I dusted off the top.

"What the—" I looked up at Jake. The setting sun reflected on the cover of a metal treasure box.

"What's the matter, Elliot?" Cassie asked. "Isn't that the box?"

"It's a treasure box all right, but it isn't the one we buried yesterday."

"This is so cool," Jake said. "I feel like we're on an archeological expedition."

I just shook my head. He helped me pull the box out of the hole. It was the same type of blue and silver tin box that I had, but it was way more rusted and dented than mine.

"How did it get so old in one night?" Jake asked. Cassie and I just looked at him. "Never mind," he squeaked.

"Open it, Elliot. Hurry," Cassie said.

I tried the top, but the latch was completely stuck. Cassie handed me a screwdriver from the tool bag, and I pried it until the top budged. The cover was so rusty and dented, that we had to yank it really hard. Jake was pulling and I was pushing when the top cranked open and Jake tumbled backward into the dirt.

"What's inside?" he yelled, while picking himself up.

The three of us held our breath as we leaned over and looked into the box. In the dimming light of day, we saw what was inside. I reached in. "It's a key," I said, picking it up. It was an old-fashioned kind of brass or copper key on a giant gold key ring.

"There's a nametag on it. What does it say?" Cassie asked. "Can you read it?"

Engraved in the gold tag, I could make out the worn letters, *V. DiStonaccio.* We wondered who the heck V. DiStonaccio was and what that key was for. And why had it been buried in my grandparents' backyard in a box that looked exactly like mine?

"Boys," my grandmother called out from the back door. "It's getting a little dark. Why don't you start cleaning up," she said, coming around the corner. "Oh, Cassie dear, I'm sorry, I didn't know you were here too. What on earth are you kids doing?"

"Hi, Mrs. Stone," Cassie greeted her.

"I'll clean up now and we'll be right in," I said. I didn't want my grandmother to see the box or the key. I got my purple notebook and added another piece of evidence:

9. Mystery treasure box with key—V. DiStonaccio

We were all a little stunned. First, we started off checking out a creepy statue and wanting to bury a treasure, then the talk of dungeons, then we stumbled upon the secret, freaky, mini door, then Cassie comes up with this shrunken head info and gravel delivery and now this. What the heck? This mission was turning out to be a lot more involved than we originally thought.

"I have to get home, guys. It's getting dark," Cassie said. "But, I have an idea. I'll look up that name and see what I can come up with. Besides, I have to get that shrunken head research out of my head. Maybe V. DiStonaccio was someone who lived here before your grandparents. I'll report back to you guys as soon as I have something."

"Okay. Jake and I will try to snoop around when we go inside."

"We will?" Jake whimpered.

"It looks like we might not be solving the mystery of the shrunken head, but the mystery of the backyard treasure—or maybe both!"

Jake moaned, holding his head this time. "Oh no! How do you get me into these things?" He pretended to cry and fell backward onto the dirt again.

After Cassie left, we went inside. There wasn't much time because it was getting late and we had school the next day. But I figured we could choke down a few oatmeal cookies and find a way to get a peek in the basement again.

"Where's Grandpa?" I asked.

"Oh, he's fiddling around with something I'm sure. You know your grandfather. He's like a little kid. Here, you boys have a few cookies, and Grandpa will drive you around the corner so you don't have to ride your bikes in the dark."

"Okay, Gram, thanks." She walked into the den and we could hear their muffled voices. I thought she was asking Grandpa to drive us home. Then Jake and I heard what he said. "Frannie, do you want me to take them now? I'm working in the dungeon. I've gotta cut down a few more heads."

My eyes sprang out of my head. "Cut down a few more heads?" I whispered to Jake in terror. "Did you hear that? He's going to the dungeon again." Then we heard him say, "Oh, Frannie, the necks are all corked."

That was it. The color drained from my face, down my arms and out through my toes. "The necks are all corked?" My voice crackled. "Did you hear that? He's cutting down heads and putting corks in the necks."

Jake and I looked at each other and choked. Pleh! Cookies and milk went spewing all over the place. "Holy crud!" The chairs screeched as we frantically pushed ourselves away from the table. "It's okay, Gram, I yelled out. It's not too dark. We'll ride together." And the two of us grabbed our stuff and hightailed it to the door.

"He didn't just say that! He didn't just say that! He didn't just say that!" I chanted down the driveway.

"What the heck?" Jake shouted, when he could finally catch his breath. "What the heckin' heck?"

We jumped on our bikes and took off, neither one of us looking back. I don't know about Jake's heart, but mine was starting to malfunction. It's not supposed to beat like that—like a bass drum on caffeine.

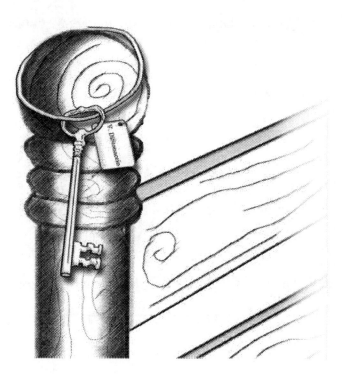

CHAPTER SIX

Big Bad Stone

I had a hard time concentrating on my homework that night. Every time I started to write, my mind drifted back to my grandfather. What was he doing? What did that creepy statue really mean? What was up with the gravel? And was he really cutting down heads in the dungeon? I started to feel a little nauseous. These clues were adding up to something, but what? A cold sweat beaded up on my stomach and my neck got all prickly. I felt gross. I put my pen down, folded my arms on my knees, and rested my head for a minute. I had to regroup. I knew I probably should have given Jake a call to set up a meeting for the next day at school, but I was beat. That's when I realized I hadn't written down the last clue in my purple notebook. That bizarre scene at my grandmother's house had me and Jake so freaked out, we went crazy and took off.

I picked my head up and looked around for my backpack. Then, I grabbed my purple notebook and added:

10. Grandpa said he was cutting down the heads and the necks were corked.

It made my skin crawl just writing the words. Then I saw the rusty cover of the treasure box we found sticking out of the open zipper. The design was almost identical to mine.

How could that be? I kept thinking. I examined it again.

Then I opened the box and studied the name V. DiStonaccio.

Who was that? I held the nametag tightly while I thought.

Then, bam! My bedroom door busted open.

"Ahhh!" I fell over.

"Eeeeek!" Sammy screamed.

"Do you mind?" I grabbed my heart. It was on shaky

ground already. I didn't need anything else that day.

"You have to take a shower, Elliot. I just took a bath.

It's your turn now. Mom said," she continued. "Mom

SAID," she repeated, singing the words this time.

"A little privacy please!" I shouted. She wasn't get-

ting the hint. So I put the key back in the box and started to

stand up.

"What's that?" Sammy started nosing around. "Was

that a key? That was a weird key. Was it a key? Where'd ya

get it?" She didn't even take a breath between questions.

"It's nothing. It's a long story. I'm going to take a shower. Just stay out of my room, please."

She folded her arms and marched away in a huff. I felt kinda bad so I called out to her in the hallway, and she turned back to look at me. I made some goofy face that made her smile, and then I said, "At least I said *please* this time." She giggled and went into her room.

"Whew!" Now I could take a shower and not worry about her. I had enough on my mind without worrying about Sammy tattling on me.

The water felt like a warm blanket on my neck. "Brrr," I shivered loudly as the cold chill left me and the steam filled up the room. It had been one of the strangest days I'd ever had. But the day wasn't over yet. While I was drying off, I heard footsteps on the stairs.

"Elliot, you have to call Cassie back. She left a message while you were in the shower."

"Okay, Mom. I'll be right down." I ran downstairs into the kitchen and grabbed the phone. Mom was putting Tommy's pajamas on. I love those little fuzzy, feety things he wears. I was making googly faces at him when Cassie answered the phone.

"Hey it's me, what's up?" I said.

"I did a genealogy search on Italian surnames," she said.

"In English, please?" I asked her. Sometimes, she's on a totally different planet. I never get those rocket-scientist types. She thrives on this stuff.

"It means the origin of the name, knucklehead."

"Oh yeah, okay. So get to the point," I said.

Then she started to tell me what she had learned about the name.

"Di, is a prefix, meaning, 'of' or 'from' and it usually relates to the father's side. Then the last part, 'accio,' usually means 'big' or 'bad.' So this name we came across on that

tag means, 'from the big, bad stone.' This HAS to be connected to your family somehow," she insisted. "Father's side,
Stone. You get it?"

"Holy crud! Wait. Let me think. So someone who
used to live in my grandparents' house had that key and
buried it in the yard, in the same box that I have? And the
name means big, bad Stone?"

"Yep!" Cassie said.

That was the last thing I remembered before I passed
out cold. The next morning, I came down for breakfast and
my mom asked me how my head was. By then, I was fine.

"What happened, Mom? Last thing I remember, I
was talking to Cassie."

"You fainted, Elliot. That was strange. Maybe you
were a little dizzy from the shower. See how you feel today.
You better take it easy."

Breakfast was quiet. Sammy was still up in her room
getting ready for school and Tommy was in his bouncy seat

swatting at a hanging clown. I watched as his tiny arm made short, jerky movements trying to reach it. No coordination yet. "We have to work on those little triceps," I told him. "We gotta get you jacked." He gurgled some spit at me and gummed a smile.

Later, I met Cassie and Jake in the hallway in front of our class. We still had a few minutes before Mrs. Pendleton would be there.

"Did you tell Jake about the name?" I asked Cassie.

They both nodded at the same time. "Yeah."

"So what does all this mean? Let's piece it together," I started. I was laying out all the scenarios. Most of them linked back to my grandfather. The shrunken head was his. He had the gravel delivered. He made the comments. And our family name was connected to the key. "But what about the secret mini door?"

"You mean *aside* from the fact it's in your grandfather's house?" Jake reminded me sarcastically.

"Okay," I admitted. "I guess that's connected to him too. The halls were starting to empty out, so I knew the morning announcements were about to begin. "But what about the name, even if it does mean big, bad Stone, the first initial said V. And my grandfather's name is Jimmy. So it can't be him."

"Yeah, but it could be a relative," Cassie added. "I think we need to find out what the key goes to and that would help us put two and two together."

"I don't want to put two and two together. I hate math," Jake said.

We decided, as much as it freaked us out, we would have to get back to my grandparents' house and do some investigation.

"Do we have to?" Jake complained. "Can't we just say your grandfather makes shrunken heads and stay away from him forever?"

"I don't think that would work. You're not going to bail on me now, are you?" I asked.

"No," Jake gave in.

He put his hand out and we all shook on it again, just in time for the morning announcements. We dashed inside when we saw Mrs. Pendleton's head turn the corner.

Later that night, I was lying on my bed doing math homework. The key sat next to my notebook distracting me from long division. Solving the mystery was ten times more interesting than math homework, for sure. I picked it up and looped the gold ring around my finger, staring at the engraved name— DiStonaccio. *Could that name have something to do with me?* I wondered.

CHAPTER SEVEN

Heritage Day

"Oh, great!" I said. "Another project? Just what I need!" Mrs. Pendleton handed out packets to everyone. Apparently, the whole entire fourth grade was doing a unit about heritage and we were going to have a Heritage Day Celebration in the cafeteria in a few weeks. Everyone had to write a report or make a poster about our family history, like a family tree or old pictures and stuff. On top of that, Mrs. Pendleton asked everyone to bring in a special food representing his or her family traditions. "I'll be signing my mom up for this one," I said to Mrs. Pendleton. Everyone laughed.

"Jake," I whispered to him, rolling my eyes. "This stinks. Now how are we gonna solve our little problem?"

"Oh well, I guess we'll have to put it on hold until Heritage Day is over," Jake suggested, hoping I would buy into that crazy idea.

"What? Nice try, Jake," I bounced back at him. This assignment was the last thing I needed. I don't know anything about my family history. "This is gonna be too much like work," I said to Jake. All of a sudden, a piece of crumpled up paper hit me in the head. "Ouch, what was that?" Cassie was waving at me. "What did ya do that for?"

"Don't worry, Elliot. I'll help you with the Heritage Day stuff. It's a breeze," Cassie said. "You just have to ask your grandparents about your family background — like an interview. That'll be a good way to get back into their house for more clues too. Think of it as an opportunity to get more information and quit moaning!"

"Good thinking. You might be right." She did have a point. We needed a way back into my grandparents' house to snoop without seeming suspicious, and this could really work to our advantage.

Jake nodded. "I hate to admit it, Cassie, but you're a genius."

"Thank you," she said with a smug little smile.

"Oh and by the way, Cass," I added, "you need to work on your modesty." We all cracked up.

Now I had to get the wheels in motion. I would bring it up at dinner tonight and see if I could set up a time to meet at my grandparents' house. But I had to figure a way to include Jake and Cassie in this too.

I walked home from school to clear my head. Sometimes the bus is so loud, and besides, it takes twice as long to get home with all those stops. It was nice to actually walk into a quiet house this time. Sammy was on the bus so I had a few minutes of peace. "Mom," I called out. "I'm home."

She turned the corner with Tommy in her arms. "Hi honey, how was school?"

"Give me that big guy," I said to her, dropping my backpack on the floor and grabbing Tommy. "School was good."

"Put your backpack away," she said as she handed him over.

"Uh huh." Tommy squealed with excitement as I bounced him up and down on my hip. He grabbed my nose and twisted it. "Ouch! Man, those little nails are sharp," I said to my mom. "You'd better clip these babies!" Tommy continued pulling at my lips, gurgling and blabbing something that seemed very important. "You've got a lot to say, little fella. Only thing is, I haven't figured out baby talk yet," I said as I stuck him in his little bouncy chair.

"So, I have this project coming up—" I started.

"Oh," my mom interrupted. "What kind of project?"

"Some Heritage Day thing. It's stupid."

"That's not stupid, Elliot. It'll be so interesting — finding out about your family background and heritage. You'll have fun doing this one."

"I will? I don't know anything about our family history. It's boring."

"Boring? Elliot, this family is far from boring. Talk to your father later. He'll have lots to tell you."

"Like what?" I said with total disinterest.

"Well, for instance, our last name. It wasn't always Stone. Over the past few generations, it was changed."

As soon as she said that, my ears perked up. "Our name was changed? From what?" My heart picked up a few beats. *Please don't say DiStonaccio. Please don't say DiStonaccio,* I thought, waiting for her answer.

"I'm not exactly sure, but it was some long Italian name with 'acci,' or 'icci,' something like that. You'll have to ask Dad when he gets home.

"Holy crud!" I blurted without thinking. I knew at that very instant the key we had found belonged to my grandfather. *He must be V. DiStonaccio,* I thought. My toes went numb and tingly, and a loud hum buzzed through my head. *But what the heck did that key go to?* I thought some more. Plans began racing through my head. I had to talk to Jake and Cassie.

"What is it, Elliot?" my mom asked.

"Uh, nothing. I'm gonna go upstairs and do homework. Then I'll ask dad when he gets home from work."

"Good idea, *for a change*," my mom said, smiling. "I'm going to walk down to the bus stop with Tommy and wait for your sister."

"Okay," I said as I grabbed a package of cookies, picked up my backpack and went upstairs.

I pulled out my homework and put the Heritage Day information on the side. I moved around some papers, rearranged my social studies homework, looked at the math problems and finally decided that I couldn't concentrate. So, I picked up my walkie-talkie to beep Jake. Before he even answered, I could hear the static starting, so I turned it off and ran down the hall to my parents' bedroom. They had a phone in there. I quickly called Jake.

"Hello?"

"Jake, this is sick! Our mission has taken a serious turn," I shouted into the phone. "I'm doing my homework and I can't really talk but you have to call Cassie and tell her this."

"What? What could have possibly happened between the time we left school and now?" he asked me.

"I just found out from my mother, that my last name, Stone, was changed at some point from a big long Italian name that sounded like 'acci' or 'icci.' How's that for a hot piece of information?"

"No way! Elliot, you can't be serious! That means—"

"I know exactly what that means. It means my grandfather is probably 'big, bad Stone' and he's been shrinking heads in his dungeon."

Jake was silent. "Jake, are you still there?"

"Yeah, I'm here. I don't think I feel so good," he answered quietly.

"Can you call Cassie and tell her the latest piece of information? I'll add this clue to the notebook and then I'm gonna see if we can get over to my grandparents' house. I want to know what that key goes to. But first I have to talk to my dad and see what our name really used to be. Maybe my mom was wrong." I was hoping with all my might that she was wrong, but I had a funny feeling. Jake promised to call Cassie and take care of that for me. I opened my purple notebook and added more clues:

11. Stone name changed from long Italian name. It could be DiStonaccio.

Then, I finished my homework even though it was really hard to concentrate. I didn't want to make the same mistake I made last year when I messed up my science project because I wasn't paying attention. I was lucky Mrs. Pendleton gave me a chance to do it over. And that was only because I was having a new baby brother. She doesn't give second chances too often.

"Elliot, Dad's home. C'mon down for dinner," my mom called up the stairs.

"I'm coming," I shouted back. I knew this was going to be interesting. I took a couple of deep breaths, shook myself and headed down to the kitchen.

I was quiet during dinner, but not by choice. First my dad talked about work, then my mom told him all about Tommy. And getting a word in between Sammy's long-winded stories was nearly impossible.

"Oh, Elliot, tell Dad about your Heritage Day project."

Here we go, I thought. I explained the whole thing again to my dad and that's when the plot thickened. "So, Dad, Mom said our name didn't always used to be Stone. Is that true?" I asked him, hoping not to get the answer I knew was coming.

"Yep. Well, it has been Stone for quite some time, but, yes that's true," my dad started. I put my fork down and focused on every word. "You see, your great-grandfather, Grandpa's father, came to the United States from Italy when he was a teenager.

He wasn't answering my question. "So what did our name used to be?" I asked again.

"It was DiStonaccio," he said. The name rolled off his tongue like he was the pizza guy at Mama Mia's.

It took all my self-control not to say anything. I didn't want him to know I knew the name. "Wow, that's long," was all I could come up with. Sometimes, I amaze myself with my stupidity.

"Yeah, it was long, but back in Italy, the names went by the family business or town they were from. Our family was in the masonry business. You know, cement, brick laying, things of that nature, and the 'Di' means—"

"I know, it means 'of' or 'from,'" I interrupted. Lucky thing Cassie gave me that info.

"Exactly, Elliot. It means 'from the family of Stone.' That's why my father shortened it to Stone before he got married. Stone made the most sense."

At that point, I couldn't swallow another bite of food. The last shred of hope I held on to was that my grandfather's name was Jimmy, so the "V" could still be someone else.

But that shred didn't last very long. "Anything else I don't know, any other name changes?" I fished for more info. *I must be crazy*, I thought.

"Yeah. As a matter of fact, Grandpa's name is really Vincent James, well, Vincenzo to be exact. He never liked Vincenzo so he's been called Jimmy as long as I can remember."

That was the last piece of information I did not want to hear. The little hairs on my scalp tingled. My weak and weary heart started malfunctioning again.

"You'll have to go talk to Grandpa," my dad said. "He'll give you a ton of information for your project. You'll be amazed. You can go over on Sunday and pick his brain."

Oh, gross, pick his brain? I thought. *Isn't there a better way of saying that?*

"Yeah, I'm amazed all right," I said, trying to stay calm. Now I knew beyond the shadow of a doubt that the mysterious key belonged to my grandfather and all that shrunken head talk and gravel being delivered was directly tied to him. There was more here than meets the eye. My grandfather had to be evil. I knew it, but how could I NOT have known it until now? My brain was scrambled. I mean, all circuits were busy.

"Dad, do you think Jake and Cassie could come with me? We're all working on Heritage Day projects," I asked.

"I don't see why not. Just check with Grandma and Grandpa first. You could probably go over early and do the work before we eat dinner."

I knew my grandmother would say yes. I called Jake as soon as I found out and we conferenced with Cassie. We set up the meeting for twelve o'clock sharp on Sunday.

"Holy cow, Elliot! I can't believe it," Jake said in amazement. "Do you really think he's been shrinking heads all this time?"

"I don't know what to think," I answered. I was still in shock.

"I TOLD you, Elliot!" Cassie added. "I knew this had something to do with your family! I just knew it! But there's just one thing..."

"What's that?" Jake and I asked at the same time.

"Well, if your grandfather is as evil as you think, wouldn't you have noticed a shrunken head before now?"

"You would think, wouldn't ya? We could sit here and question this all night long. It's no use. Let's wait until Sunday," I suggested.

"Good idea. You're right, Elliot," Cassie said. "We'll talk to your grandparents and take notes for the project—"

"Then we'll find a way back down to the basement and do some investigating."

"Elliot, wait a minute!" Cassie blurted. "You just said it!"

"Said what?"

"What now?" Jake chimed in.

"Do you think the key goes to the mini-door in their basement?" Cassie asked excitedly.

"THAT'S IT!" I shouted. "Jake, did you hear that?"

"How could I not? You practically broke my ear drums, man."

"I'll bet you're right, Cassie," I said. "That key probably goes to the freaky secret mini-door."

"Holy crud! Double holy crud!" was all Jake managed to say.

"Now we just have to find out exactly what is behind that door," I said with confidence.

"We do?" Jake asked.

"Yeah, we do!"

"I was afraid you were gonna say that."

CHAPTER EIGHT

The Freaky Secret Mini-Door

With one foot on the curb and one on the pedal, I

waited on the corner for Jake and Cassie. I tapped my

fingers on the handlebars and checked my watch. It was ten

minutes to twelve. They would be there any minute. I was

about to beep Jake, when I saw Cassie's red jacket from the

distance. A second later, I saw Jake. We pulled up to each other and parked our bikes. "Let's make sure we have everything for the mission," I said.

"I have a flashlight," Cassie began, "and some oil just in case the door lock is rusted."

"Good thinking," I said. "Jake? Anything?"

"I brought me," Jake said in a high-pitched voice.

"Nice going. Good thing we have you on this mission," I teased. "Anyway, I've got my purple notebook to interview my grandfather, the Heritage Day packet, and the treasure box with the key. Is that all?" The three of us agreed we had everything we needed. It looked like we were ready to attempt the dangerous mission and get behind the secret mini-door. But first we had to interview my grandfather for the project.

The smell of spaghetti sauce greeted us at the front door. My grandmother was thrilled to dole out not one, but three, of her patented Grandma hugs.

"I'm so glad you kids are here," she said. "Jake and Cassie, you're both welcome to stay for dinner when you're through working on the project."

"Oh thanks, Mrs. Stone. I'll call my mother," Cassie answered.

"Me too," said Jake. "I wouldn't miss your spaghetti and meatballs for anything."

"Oh, how sweet," my grandmother said. "I'll go get Grandpa for you kids."

When my grandfather came into the dining room, he put a bottle of wine into the rack and sat down in the armed chair at the far end of the table with a brown envelope in his hands.

"How's everybody doing?" he asked, slapping the table loudly. "So what do you want to know?" He was ready for some storytelling. My grandfather loves to talk. I knew I had to keep the questions short or this would take us a while.

I still wanted to get into that basement and start investigating.

"So, I have this Heritage Day project to do, and I need some information about our family history," I started. The first question I could think of was, "Where did our family come from?" My grandfather took a deep breath, his eyes widened, and I had a feeling this one was going to be a long answer.

"Well," he started, raising his eyebrows. "My father came to this country from Italy in 1913—June third to be exact. He was nineteen years and had only ten dollars in his pocket."

I took notes as my grandfather was talking. Jake and Cassie listened. I think Cassie was really intrigued by the whole story. And, actually, I was kind of interested too.

He told us how his father left Palermo, Sicily, on the S.S. Indiana and came to this country without knowing anyone. Now that's what I call brave — going to a strange country where you can't speak the language, all by yourself.

"What's the S.S. Indiana?" I asked.

"It's the ship that sailed from Italy to America," he answered, pulling open the envelope. "Here are the ship's passenger list and manifest." He showed us the old, worn documents. We could barely make out the writing.

"What's a manifest?" I asked him.

Cassie interjected and told us the manifest was where they keep a record of the passengers on board, where they came from, and a list of their belongings.

"Exactly," my grandfather said. Then he showed us the line where his father's name was: Line 38: Vincenzo Di Stonaccio.

"Wait, Grandpa. Dad said *your* name was Vincenzo," I said, looking up at Jake and Cassie.

"That's true, I'm named after him, but I never did like the name. So I use my middle name, Jimmy." The three of us looked at each other again. Then we moved over to my grandfather's side of the table to examine the documents more closely.

"Here's his signature," my grandfather pointed out.

"This is so cool!" Jake said to me. "Your great-grandfather actually signed this piece of paper?"

"Can I have a copy of this for my project?" I asked.

"Of course," my grandfather said as he pulled out more papers. "I have another set right here."

"I might actually have the best report ever," I said. Jake made a face at me. "C'mon, who else has an actual ship's manifest?" Then Cassie got the look in her eyes. I knew she was working up a question.

"So, how did you get the name Stone?" she asked my grandfather.

He told her the same story I had heard from my dad a few days earlier, about the family being in the masonry business and what the name meant. Then he told us that he was the one who had changed the name to just plain Stone.

"Why'd you do that?" I asked.

"Well, back then, if you had a very ethnic name, people would judge you. There are certain Italian stereotypes we had to endure. I decided before I married your grandmother, I would shorten the name to Stone so there would be no prejudices toward my family."

"Wow," I said. But, I was still thinking about the key. I knew Jake and Cassie were thinking what I was thinking. *The V. initial on the key ring was definitely his, and I guarantee it has to do with that mini-door we found downstairs.*

"This is great, Grandpa, thanks," I said as I scribbled down the last few words in my notebook. So I'm really Elliot DiStonaccio?"

"I suppose so," my grandfather answered.

Then Jake started calling me "Elliato" and we all burst into laughter.

"We're gonna take a break now," I said. "Can you help me with the names for my family tree?"

"Sure," my grandfather said. "After dinner. I have to go take care of a few things first."

The three of us watched him walk out of the dining room toward the kitchen. We listened carefully to see if he said anything. Nothing. But we heard the side door slam. He definitely went outside.

"Now's our chance," I said. "Let's move."

"Hey, Grandma," I said, as we walked through the kitchen. I went straight to the saucepot, picked up the cover and took a big whiff. "Mmm. Smells great! Can we go downstairs for a minute? I think I left my video game down there when we got the peaches last Sunday."

"Of course. While you're down there, do me a favor and grab a few more cans of peaches. It's hard for me to go up and down those stairs."

"You got it, Gram," I said, stealing a meatball out of the frying pan. "You want half?" I offered Cassie and Jake. I knew Cassie would say no. Jake was already holding a piece of bread waiting for his half. He smacked his lips and we made our way down the hall to the basement door.

"You go first," Jake said, with a big mouthful.

Cassie pushed the two of us out of the way. "We'll never get anything done with you two babies. I'll go first!"

"Sheesh, I feel hurt," Jake pouted.

Cassie started down the stairs. Jake and I followed. We directed her to where the canning shelf was and stayed close behind.

"Are there any lights down here?" she asked.

"Oh, yeah, right here." I jumped up to reach the string on the light bulb above us. POP! The bulb blew out as soon as I pulled the string. "Oh, great! You still have that flashlight, Cassie?" I asked. She handed me the light and I aimed it over to the shelf. "See the door?" I said, showing her.

Cans rattled and boxes fell over as the three of us struggled to move the shelf away from the wall. "Shhh, we're gonna get caught," I said.

We got up close to look at the lock. The door barely reached my thighs, so we had to kneel down. Cassie grabbed her spray bottle and squirted oil into the keyhole. Then I opened my backpack, took out the treasure box and lifted the lid. "Here, spray the key too," I told her. Then, just as we were ready to try the lock, I heard the doorbell ring upstairs. I knew my parents had just arrived because Sammy's voice was echoing all the way down here. "We have to hurry, guys. They'll be calling us in a few minutes."

The key and the keyhole were exactly the same shape. They had to go together. I put the key in slowly. My heart was pounding. Jake wiped sweat off his forehead. Even Cassie had little beads of sweat on her upper lip, and she never sweats. I tried to turn the key, but it was jammed. It wouldn't turn at all. "Help me out," I motioned to Jake. He put his hand on top of mine and we tried again. Still, nothing. Cassie sprayed a little more oil into the lock while we were turning and suddenly, BAM! the key turned and the door flew open. I went flying into a miniature stairwell with Jake on top of me. There were three steps on top, but then the stairs made a sharp turn to the right. I was headfirst looking down into the eerie stairwell.

"Are you okay?" Cassie poked her head through the doorway. It was pitch dark, and cold clammy air grabbed onto us. Instantly, we were overtaken by a horrible stench.

"Ew," Jake covered his mouth. "It smells like shrunken heads. This must be the dungeon. Let's get out of here."

"No way!" Cassie blocked the doorway. "We've come too far to turn around now. We're not leaving until we get to the bottom of this."

CHAPTER NINE

The Dungeon

Jake and I picked ourselves up, well, as *up* as we

could be. After all, we were crouched in that dark, mini-

stairwell. Cassie stayed close behind us with her hand on my shoulders. The three of us began to slowly creep down the stairs—one creaky step after another. I batted at a few cobwebs draping across the stairwell and spit out the ones that were caught in my mouth.

"Eeek!" Cassie waved her arms around frantically.

"Shh," I said, spitting some more. "We don't want anyone to hear us."

"But I hate spiders," she whispered back.

"Not as much as I hate people screaming in my ears!" Jake said.

We kept going. As we got deeper, the air in the stairwell got colder and the odor got stronger. Our breathing was perfectly synchronized as the three of us inhaled and exhaled on the way down.

"Is that a curtain?" Cassie asked, pointing to the bottom of the stairwell.

"It looks like one. Let's see what's behind it," I said.

"After you." Jake motioned for me to go first—the big chicken!

At this point my heart began to short circuit. I didn't think it was possible for a human heart to beat so fast. In fact, my face was pulsating and my hands began to shake uncontrollably. I thought I was going to explode. I slowly moved the heavy brown drapes to one side. Jake was leaning over my shoulder, and Cassie, leaning over his. The smell was overwhelming.

"Ugh," Jake choked. "I'm gonna die here."

Jake thought it smelled like shrunken heads, but I thought it smelled like feet.

We all covered our noses and I moved the curtain a little further. A draft of cold air swept through as I opened the curtain.

"It's freezing down here," Cassie said, shivering.

On the right side of the room, I noticed a long table with three huge pots. Cassie saw it at the same time.

"Oh, no!" she blurted. "Those pots are filled with water! Someone really IS making shrunken heads down here!"

"WHAT?" Jake shouted, jerking backwards, his head banging into the wall. "Ow! Maybe that's why it's so cold down here — to keep the heads preserved."

"Holy crud," I answered, remembering Cassie's shrunken head research and the boiling water. This really seemed like a *holy crap* moment, but I'm not allowed to curse, so *holy crud* had to do. By now, my curiosity was winning over my fear. I was sucked in. I moved a little closer to the curtain. "C'mon Jake, Cassie. Let's go in." I ducked through the curtain first and gasped at the gory sight. Jake and Cassie stopped short behind me.

"What, what is it?" Cassie asked. "Tell us what you see!"

I couldn't believe my eyes. Here I was, in this secret dungeon in my grandparents' basement, in the pitch dark and

I was looking at rows and rows of what looked like hanging miniature heads.

"J-Jake…I-I—" I tried to speak, but the words wouldn't come out. Jake pushed ahead of me and looked up.

"Ahhhhh, ahhhhh," Jake screamed. "It's the shrunken heads!" He started to run, but he didn't know which way to go. He tripped over my feet and we both went crashing down to the floor. Our arms and legs were flailing around like we were drowning. Rushing to get to our feet, we got tangled in a mess of heads—dozens of disgusting shrunken heads, swinging around on strings. Even long, shriveled up brown things were hanging too.

"Those must be the necks," I said in terror.

"Ahh, they're touching me!" Jake screamed again.

"Eeeek," Cassie squealed in crazy hysteria. "Let's get out of here."

It was worse than a PG-13 horror movie. The three of us panicked, running in different directions, when Jake fell again and crashed into one of the pots. Gallons of water came splashing down on Jake. As he thrashed around in the puddle, four more heads rolled out of the pot toward us. Everyone started screaming.

"Quick, back to the stairs!" I yelled. Suddenly, we saw a dim light go on. A dark shadowy figure moved at the far end of the room. We held our breath trying to be perfectly quiet. Then the shadowy figure spoke in a deep voice.

"What's going on down here?"

"Ahhh!" the three of us screamed again. Jake bolted for the stairs like an animal, on all fours. Cassie and I hightailed it behind him. She got to the stairs first, and just as I was about to hurl myself through the drapes, I slipped on the spilled water and landed flat on my stomach.

"C'mon, Elliot, hurry up! Hurry up!" they screamed.

The adrenaline rush must've given me super strength because I dragged myself up onto the stairwell with only my arms. My heart was thumping through my chest. All I could think about was getting the heck out of this dungeon and how could my grandfather be shrinking heads? Then all of a sudden, I felt the death grip wrap around my ankles and I screamed. Cassie leaped back down the stairs and grabbed my arm, trying to pull me loose.

"Help us, Jake," she called out.

The shadowy figure pulled me back through the curtain. I knew my life was over. The figure spoke again, as he dragged me back into the room.

"What in tar nation are you doing down here, Elliot?"

"Grandpa, is that you?"

"Who else would it be?" he said. "You kids made a bit of a mess down here, I see."

"Why do you have all these shrunken heads down here?" I asked, still lying on the floor. "Are you gonna shrink my head now, too?" My bottom lip quivered.

CHAPTER TEN

The Truth about Grandpa

"What the heck are you talking about boy?" he said, helping me up. He could see I was visibly shaken. Cassie let go of my arm and she and Jake came down closer to listen.

The Truth about Grandpa

"Why do you have all the shrunken heads hanging from the ceiling, and…and those shriveled necks?" I said, pointing up at them. "And what about those pots of water with soaking heads—it's just like in the research Cassie did. Right, Cass?" I said, turning to her. She nodded in agreement.

"I think you're getting hysterical," my grandfather said, flipping on the lights. "Calm down." He patted me on the shoulder. "This is my wine cellar. You've never been down here?"

"No. Never," I answered, wiping the dampness from my eyes.

"Come on kids, I'll give you the penny tour. But we have to make it quick, your grandmother is about to put the food on the table and I don't want to get in trouble." He walked us further into the room.

"This is where I make the provolone cheese and the dried Italian sausage, you knucklehead," he explained, looking at me. Cassie and Jake's mouths hung open.

"Cheese and sausage?" I asked him, in shock. "That's it? Cheese and sausages in a wine cellar? Then why the secret door behind the canning shelf? Why not a normal entrance, like normal people?"

"What secret door?" my grandfather asked. "Oh, you mean that little crawl space entrance you kids came through? I don't even know how you fit through there. We haven't used that little entrance since I was a kid. When my father expanded the house, he added the bunker."

"Bunker?"

"Yeah, this is like a bunker. It's a cellar below the cellar with a separate entrance. He used it as a wine cellar too. We've been doing this for generations. Originally, we used that little stairwell leading down here, but I added the outside entrance years ago. It was much easier to get to from the outside."

Jake, Cassie and I were in awe. We followed my grandfather around like little puppies as he showed us everything. It was like watching the history channel. I think my heart finally slowed to a normal beat.

Next, he walked us over to the rows of neatly hung cheeses and dried sausages. Well, most of them were neatly hung, except for the ones we tangled up during our freak-out. As I walked around, I couldn't believe my eyes. *How did I not know he was making cheese and sausage all this time?* I thought.

"Here," he said to us, cutting down one of the heads. "Try this." Cassie and I took a tiny bite and handed it to Jake.

"I'll try it, as long as it's not a shrunken head," he said, laughing.

"You see these here?" my grandfather pointed to the cheese. These have to hang for at least six months if you want good sharp provolone," he continued. "The sausages don't need as long—only about two months to age. But, in order for them to age properly, the temperature has to be just right. That's why this sub-cellar is a good place. It's nice and cold down here. Then when they're good and ready, I come and cut 'em down. That's what you eat every Sunday with your spaghetti and meatballs."

Next he walked us over to two barrels. "And, over here is where I age the wine. When it's ready, I fill the bottles and cork the necks. That's when they go upstairs."

"Whoa!" Jake said, looking at Cassie, then at me. "I don't believe it."

"This is so cool!" Cassie answered. "Elliot, you really are going to have the best Heritage Day project. Look at all this great information we uncovered."

"Well, kids," my grandfather said. "We better get our butts upstairs or your grandmother is gonna string us up for sure—no pun intended." We all started cracking up.

My grandfather cut down one more piece of cheese and one big link of dried sausage. "Here carry these up. I'll get some wine," he said. "Oh, and by the way, after dinner you kids are coming back down here to clean up this awful mess!"

"You got it, gramps!" I said with a grin. Then the three of us walked over to the real door and went up to the house for dinner.

When we got upstairs, my grandmother was putting the food on the table, my mom was feeding Tommy and my dad was reading a story to Sam.

"What took you so long? We were getting worried," my grandmother said.

"I gave them a little tour of the wine cellar, Frannie. It seems they thought I was shrinking heads down there."

"What?" my grandmother said, a little confused.

I saw my mom and dad turn to me with the usual, *what are you up to?* look in their eyes. I felt like a jerk. My face heated up with embarrassment as Jake and Cassie burst into laughter. Then I started laughing and soon everyone in the room was hysterical. My eyes were tearing and my sides started hurting. When everyone finally stopped laughing, we all took our seats around the dining room table.

"So what's the real story, Elliot?" my dad asked. "Out with it."

I got up quickly and ran to the living room. Then I came back with the shrunken head statue and began telling everyone what happened. "It all started with this creepy thing," I said, holding up the gruesome head. "We saw this statue, and then we heard Grandpa say he was going down to the dungeon to cut down some heads. We even heard him say he was corking necks and we freaked out." Everyone laughed at that part. "So," I continued, "Cassie did some research on shrunken heads — Cassie, you tell them."

"Well, I found out that a long time ago in the Amazon, certain tribes used gravel and pots of water to shrink the heads of their enemies," she added. "Then we saw the pile of gravel in your yard while we were digging up the treasure chest and we thought you were shrinking heads too."

"What treasure chest?" Sammy shouted. "I want some treasure. Is there real treasure?"

My grandfather poured the wine for the grownups explaining the woody flavor of this batch. "Oh, that gravel is for my garden," he said, nonchalantly.

"But it's fall. Who buys stuff for the garden in the fall?"

"I got a great deal on the price because it was the end of the season, but I had to take delivery now. You kids have some imagination," my grandfather said. "So, how did you open that crawl space door anyway? It's been locked for decades," he asked, passing some sausage around the table.

I pulled the key ring out of my pocket and held it up. Tommy's eyes beamed, as he tried to reach for it. "No, no, no," I said in a baby voice. "This one's mine, little fella." Tommy loves keys too.

"Elliot!" my dad said, "Where on earth did you get that? I haven't seen that key since I was a boy." He held out his hand to examine it. That's when Jake held up the treasure chest.

"It was in this."

"Wait," my dad said, excitedly. "Where did you find that? That's my box!"

"Your box?" I asked. "How can it be yours?" I explained how we buried my treasure box in the yard and when we tried to dig it up, we found this one instead.

"You're not going to believe this," Dad explained. "When I was a kid, I buried that box in the backyard with my best friend, Johnny Himmelfarb." He laughed out loud. "That's my key!" he said proudly. "You know, we never could find it again after that day," he chuckled.

"Yours?" my grandfather interrupted. "I believe that key belonged to me, long before you had it, Hubert. Did you know, that key ring and name tag are real gold?"

"Really? Real gold?" Jake chimed in, stuffing a meatball in his mouth. "You mean we dug up real treasure? Cool!"

I finished telling everyone how we saw the name on the key ring, but didn't think it was Grandpa's because I had never heard of the name DiStonaccio before, and Grandpa's name is Jimmy. Then Cassie told everyone about her genealogy search on the name.

"DiStonaccio means, 'from the big bad stone,'" she said.

"You kids spent an awful lot of time worrying for nothing," my grandmother said. "Next time just ask."

My mom agreed, as she broke off a piece of a meat-ball and gave it to Tommy. I could tell from the way he was wiggling around that he liked real food better than that mushy jar stuff.

"Cassie," my grandfather said, "you're quite the re-searcher. That's what I like to see, someone who gets to the bottom of things." Cassie blushed. "Elliot, if you'd paid half that much attention during Sunday dinners here, you might have known all of this."

"Yeah," my dad teased, "instead of flicking sesame seeds at your sister, maybe you could listen in on the conver-sation and find out a little about your family traditions and heritage."

"Who knew?" I said, laughing. "Grandpa, will you show me how to make some of that stuff down there?" I asked.

"Of course, Elliot. This is a dying art," he said, hold-ing up a piece of sausage, shaking it as he spoke. "There aren't too many people who do this anymore. You can be the next generation of Stone men who make their own Italian foods and wine. Your father never got into it."

"This is so great," Cassie said. "I learned so much to-day."

"Me too," Jake chimed in.

"I guess I won't be needing this anymore," I said, taking the purple notebook out of my back pocket. Then my mom suggested we all make a toast. Everyone held up a glass. Even Tommy waved his bottle in the air, mimicking us.

"Here's to family tradition," my mother began.

"And here's to finding my forty-year-old buried treasure," Dad chuckled.

"Wait," I said. "Here's to the best Heritage Day project ever! Thanks, Grandpa—"

"And thank heavens you're not shrinking heads down there!" shouted Jake.

Everyone cheered with laughter as we toasted. The dining room echoed with the sounds of forks pinging on plates, glasses clinking, water pouring, voices humming and bursts of laughter, and of course, an occasional squeal from Tommy.

CHAPTER ELEVEN

A Birthday Surprise

Weeks later, we were headed back to my grandpar-

ents' house for Sunday dinner. But this time, it wasn't an

ordinary Sunday dinner. This time it was a very special

dinner. It was October 20th, my birthday, and I was turning double digits.

I had been spending every Sunday with my grandfather. He taught me how to make the provolone cheese and soak it in the salt water. He showed me how to make the sausages and put them in the casings. Then, it was my job to tie the cord in a knot on all the tops. Every week, I got to climb on a step stool and hang them in rows. We were a great team. In fact, we did so well together, that my grandfather came with me to my Heritage Day celebration at school. We set up a table displaying the passenger list and manifest from the S.S. Indiana, and I hung up my family tree with the genealogy information about our name. The coolest part was our sample tray of homemade cheese and dried sausage. Grandpa and I made a big hit that day.

So, for my birthday dinner, I went to the cellar with my grandfather and helped him pick out the best cheese and the perfect sausage. I even cut 'em down myself. Then my grandfather let me put the cork in the wine and bring it upstairs. I felt like an official DiStonaccio.

My grandma invited Jake and Cassie for dinner again, since it was my birthday celebration. We ate and drank and shared funny stories. Of course, I flicked a few sesame seeds across the table at Sammy. It was still fun to annoy her. Tommy gummed Italian bread until it disintegrated into mush and Jake inhaled meatballs as usual.

Cassie engaged in sophisticated conversation with my mother and grandmother, and Jake and I fooled around with my dad.

After we finished eating dinner, my grandmother brought a cake over to the table. She lit the candles and everyone sang an off-tune "Happy Birthday." We need to work on that. It was pretty bad. I made a wish and blew out the candles, and my mom handed me a stack of cards.

"Oh yeah, money gifts, my favorite!" I opened each one, pretending to read the words and stashed the cash in my pocket. *I might finally save up enough money for a new video game*, I thought. I thanked everyone. "This was the best birthday ever!" I said, taking a piece of cake. As I gobbled the first forkful, my grandfather got up from the table, making an announcement.

"Eh hem, I have something for you, Elliot," he said. "I'll be right back." He returned a minute later, holding a gift. "Here Elliot," he said. "This is a special gift just from me."

Everyone watched as I tried to tear off the wrapping. It had a ton of tape on it, so it was nearly impossible to get open. "Nice tape job, Grandpa," I mocked.

"What is it? Elliot, Elliot, what is it?" Sammy sang.

Cassie helped me tear some of the paper. Then Jake grabbed the corner and ripped it open, roaring with laughter. The joke was on me. It was the Shrink-a-Head, Monster Candy Making Kit.

"Now we can shrink some heads for real," my grandfather said, winking at me.

"And eat 'em, too!" added Jake, with a great big smile.

Take the Elliot Quiz

1. Describe how Elliot felt during the "Trek of Doom." Have you ever had those same feelings? When?

2. Elliot couldn't part with a few items. Name three of them. Do you have a special item? Explain what makes it special to you.

3. What does Elliot hate more than anything else in the world? Is there a task you dislike? Why?

4. Describe the Sleeping Willow. Draw a picture of how you see it.

5. What picture comes to your mind when you hear the word dungeon? Now look up the word "dungeon." What is the origin of the word?

6. During the box burial, which clue caused Cassie to chew her fingernails? Describe a nail-biting experience you have had in the past.

7. Research the genealogy of your name. What did you find?

8. Describe the assignment Mrs. Pendleton handed out to her class. Would you like doing an assignment like that?

9. What did Elliot's father mean by the statement, "You can go over on Sunday and pick his brain?" Write down a few more figures of speech.

10. On which ship did Elliot's great-grandfather sail to America?

11. Do you have any relatives who came from another country? Find out more by conducting an interview. Be prepared with a list of questions.

12. How did you feel when Elliot, Jake, and Cassie stumbled on the hanging heads? What would you have done if you were there?

13. What common interest do Elliot, Mr. Stone, and Tommy share?

14. What are your special family traditions? Which traditions do you enjoy the most?

15. What joke was played on Elliot? What is the best joke you have ever played on someone?

About the Author

L.P. Chase began writing this series for her children who, being avid readers, complained, "There are no more books in the house to read." Just for fun, she created the character Elliot Stone, and the book took on a life of its own. Chase plans on continuing the series and is in the process of writing the third installment, *Elliot Stone and the Mystery of the Summer Vacation Sea Monster.* She's also penned, *Today is Tuesday,* and *I Kiss the Moon,* a collection of poetry. In addition to writing, L.P. Chase enjoys spending time with her three children, exercising, baking, and reading. Chase resides with her family in Smithtown, New York.